The Invisible Boy

The Invisible Boy

Hazel Townson

Illustrated by Tony Ross

Andersen Press
London

First published in 2002 by
Andersen Press Limited,
20 Vauxhall Bridge Road, London SW1V 2SA
www.andersenpress.co.uk

Reprinted 2002, 2003

British Library Cataloguing in Publication Data available
ISBN 1 84270 105 3

Phototypeset by Intype London Ltd
Printed and bound in Great Britain by
Mackays of Chatham Ltd, Chatham, Kent

Contents

For the staff and pupils of
St. Augustine's Catholic Primary School, Weymouth

First Encounter
The Magic Key

Have you ever felt like nobody,
Just a tiny speck of air,
When everyone's around you
And you are just not there?

'Being Nobody' by Karen Crawford, aged 9

Gary Gardner had begun to suspect that he was turning invisible. Nobody seemed to notice him any more.

He reckoned this was the fault of the icy cold key he now had to wear round his neck. That key must be magic. Black magic. There was no escape from it. When he ran it tapped against his chest with a sinister rhythm. When he fidgeted at his desk it slithered around beneath his shirt, reminding him that he was nothing and nobody. Even when he sat perfectly still it lay like a warning finger on his heart. That key had changed his life, and not for the better.

One day last winter there had been a massive row at home, after which Gary and his dad had left. The row had had something to do with supermarket boss, Mr Slopton, bringing boxes of chocolates to Gary's mum. Gary didn't think that was any reason for Dad and himself to pack their bags and rush off in the car to Gran's house by the sea. But then, nobody asked Gary's opinion. Nobody cared that he'd had to leave his bike behind and all his video games and his Manchester United strip. He'd even lost one of his pyjama tops in the upheaval.

They'd hardly settled in at Gran's when she suddenly had a heart attack and died. Dad blamed this on the shock of hearing about Mr Slopton's chocolates. Gary reckoned they must have been very expensive chocolates for everyone to make such a fuss. He wondered if maybe Mr Slopton had stolen them.

Gary had been fond of his gran and was very sad about her death, but he wasn't allowed to go to the funeral. His dad gave him money for the pictures instead. After the funeral Gran's house belonged to Dad, so now that was where the two of them lived, and Gary went to a new and very different school – always with the black magic key round his neck.

The school was called St Elspeth's-of-the-Storm, as it was built on a rocky bit of coastline famous for shipwrecks. All the children there were great readers. Their mums and dads kept on turning up at school to make sure their children got more and more difficult reading books. Gary's dad never went to the school at all, though Gary's reading book seemed to be more difficult than anyone else's. Worse still, the children all

11

had their own special friends and didn't need a new one, especially one who was fast disappearing. The teachers didn't seem to need a new pupil either, for although Gary's hand shot up often in class he was never invited to speak.

In this new life Gary had to wear his key all the time. He even wore it in bed at night, in case he should forget to pick it up in the morning. After school each day that key let him into an empty house. He was supposed to have a minder, old Mrs Flyte at the next house along, but she rarely moved from the armchair in front of her television screen. Mrs Flyte was deaf and didn't even hear when Gary called on her, let alone give any sign of having seen him. His visits to her house grew shorter and shorter until in the end all he did was to pop his head round her door in a token gesture before slinking off home.

Gran's house was perched on the cliff-top and always echoed with the mournful sound of the sea. Sometimes the sea grew angry

and the sound became louder and very frightening. Bits of the house would rattle, creak and shudder. At times like this Gary hid in the cubby-hole under the stairs.

Gary usually had the house to himself for a good part of the evening, as his dad had begun staying later and later at his office. Dad even worked Saturday mornings now, and on Sundays he stayed in bed late, then hid behind the newspapers or tinkered with the car. Gary couldn't help noticing that his dad hardly spoke at all these days, and when he did it was as though he were speaking to himself.

Maybe he can't see me properly either, thought Gary. He took to peering anxiously through the mirror in the hall to make sure he was still there, but one day the mirror fell off the wall and broke.

Seven years' bad luck!

Dad threw the pieces in the dustbin. That left only Dad's shaving mirror in the bathroom which hung too high for Gary and was usually steamed up anyway.

14

Today the key felt colder than ever. It was tapping little coughs out of Gary's chest as he trudged along the cliff-top towards school. There was a strong wind blowing off the sea which made him pull up his hood and hunch down inside his jacket.

Suddenly he spotted a figure in the distance: a squat, silvery figure like some burly knight-in-armour standing very still on the

headland. Just a trick of the light, no doubt, yet it created the strange suggestion of some being from another world, alien or angel. Then, just as suddenly, the creature vanished.

That was when Gary had his great idea. He would vanish, too. That would prove once and for all whether he was growing invisible or not. If people didn't notice his presence, then maybe they would notice his absence. They would have to come looking for him. And when they tracked him down, then he would know for certain that he was still visible, still important, still wanted, still THERE.

It was a wonderful idea. Gary performed a little skip of triumph until the key calmed him down with a smart warning tap across the ribs.

Second Encounter
Alien on a Headland

Naturally, Gary wanted to be tracked down. It would be terrible if he hid himself away and nobody was able to spot him, however hard they looked. Perhaps he ought to make sure first that his invisibility hadn't already gone too far?

Worried by this idea, he decided to try making contact once more with some of his classmates before he laid any further plans.

Jess Devine and Lucy Jones, the two girls who sat at the table in front of Gary, seemed the most approachable. Jess had actually smiled in his direction once, so perhaps she had keener eyesight than the rest.

At break that morning Gary's big chance came. Jess and Lucy were sitting alone in a corner of the playground giggling over a comic. Gary screwed up his courage and went to talk to them.

It wasn't easy. What on earth could he say? He found himself blushing and his tongue seemed to be coated in glue, but eventually he brought up the subject which was much on his mind:

'Er – I was wondering – er – do you two like chocolates?'

The girls didn't appear to have heard him. Neither of them looked up.

'I – er – I know how to get some for free,' Gary improvised wildly. 'Chocolates, I mean.'

Visualising Mr Slopton's offerings, he added: 'Posh ones in big boxes. Very expensive.'

Jess turned over a page and pointed at something. Lucy followed her finger, totally absorbed. Could they not see or hear him?

Matters seemed to be worse than he'd thought.

'These are really – er – really special chocolates,' Gary blundered on desperately. 'Out of this world.'

Gary knew only too well how special chocolates could be. Chocolates could change whole lives. They'd certainly changed his life once, so maybe they could again. Girls were supposed to like chocolates, weren't they? To his own surprise he began to weave them into an amazing story beginning with the figure he had seen on the headland that morning. Anything to make this pair look at him.

'It's this stranger in a silver suit who's giving them away. Looks like somebody out of "Star Wars" . . .' Gary struggled on.

The plan wasn't working, though. The girls didn't even lift their heads from the comic.

'. . . And do you know why he looks like that? Because he's an ALIEN,' the poor lad blurted out at last. 'From Mars or somewhere.' (Come to think of it, the figure *had* looked like an alien in that silver get-up.) 'Landed on the dunes in a SPACESHIP!'

Well, if that didn't do the trick he didn't know what would. Yet perhaps he had gone too far this time, for the two girls collapsed in an uncontrollable fit of giggles. The trouble was, poor Gary couldn't be sure whether they were laughing at him or at the comic.

Before he could say any more they both leapt to their feet and staggered away, holding onto each other in a state of total hysteria.

What had Gary proved by this encounter? Had those girls seen him and simply chosen to ignore him? He couldn't be sure. Yet he knew now that he desperately needed to find out the truth. He couldn't go on like this; he must definitely put his vanishing plan into action.

Strangely enough, once he had made that decision the magic key already felt lighter and less cold.

Third Encounter
An Empty House

Robert Gardner arrived home late as usual. He was working longer and longer hours as the weeks went by and was beginning to feel more at home in his office than he did in his mother's house despite having spent his childhood there. He dropped his keys on the hall table and called upstairs.

'Gary! Fry-up or take-away?'

Silence.

Robert knew perfectly well that his son would be up there in his room, because Gary hated staying at Mrs Flyte's and never waited to be collected.

The lad was sulking, then. Not surprising, as the two of them rarely spoke to each other these days. The situation had grown so uncomfortable that last night Robert had decided guiltily to make more effort with the lad. He must stop working late and spend more time at home.

When Gary and his dad had first arrived here the plan had been for Gran to keep an eye on Gary until things were sorted out. Yet now, when there was no Gran to help, things were getting out of hand. Deaf old Mrs Flyte was no proper substitute and better arrangements would have to be made.

Meantime, in an attempt to heal the rift, Robert had bought a present for Gary. That afternoon he had taken time off work to attend a special sale at a costume-hire shop which was closing down and had bought his son a lightsabre. Gary would like that; he was a great fan of Obi Wan Kenobi. Robert planned to give him the present after supper.

Throwing off his jacket, Robert walked

through into the kitchen. Because of attending the sale he had had no time to do the shopping, so they would have to manage with whatever was in the fridge. Once Gary caught the whiff of food he'd be downstairs like a shot.

Robert laid slices of bacon on the grill, remembering with a pang the wonderful meals his wife used to cook, which that low-life Slopton would now be tucking into.

He added a couple of sausages and called upstairs again.

'Right then, wash your hands and come and lay the table.'

Appetising smells began to drift through into the hall. Robert collected the frying-pan plus a couple of eggs. His wife, with her carefully-balanced menus, would have deplored this kind of meal, but by eight o'clock in the evening supper had to be something quick. Poor old Gary must be starving.

Robert picked up the tongs and turned the bacon. One of the sausages rolled from

the grill to the floor. At the same moment he stepped back to avoid the spitting bacon and slipped on the sausage, throwing up his arms and sending several items clattering from the worktop to the floor.

Robert lost his temper.

'Gary!' he thundered, forgetting his new peacemaking resolve. 'Get down here NOW and lay this table! I can't be expected to do everything myself.'

Still no answer. The boy must have heard all that noise.

'One last chance!' Robert bellowed. 'If you aren't down here in two seconds flat, I'll eat the lot myself.'

He didn't mean it, though. When the meal was ready Robert marched upstairs to collect his son.

The boy's room was empty.

No school-bag; no kicked-off boots; no uniform blazer and tie thrown down on the chair as usual. No sign, in fact, that Gary had ever come home at all that day.

His meal forgotten, Robert ran straight over to Mrs Flyte's. Perhaps they'd both got absorbed in a television programme? Or maybe the lad was ill and the old lady had tucked him up on the sofa? But by the time he realised that Mrs Flyte hadn't seen Gary at all that day and knew nothing, Robert was in a state of sheer **blind panic**.

Rushing back home, he charged from room to room, crashing doors open and yelling Gary's name as he searched the house. He included the garden, the garage, the tool shed. When all that failed he even got the ladder out and went up into the loft. Kids could get up to all sorts of daft tricks if the fancy took them.

He finally had to admit that the boy was nowhere on the premises. Was he so fed up that he'd run away? Back to his mother's maybe? Or was it something much more serious?

Struck with sudden dread, he grabbed the telephone and dialled the school's number, but of course it was much too late; there was nobody left at school by that time. He followed this with a call to his wife but got no reply there either. She was probably out on the town with fat slob Slopton. Slopton had a mobile phone, but Robert didn't know the number.

What about Gary's friends, then? Robert

couldn't remember his son mentioning any friends since the move to Gran's, but he rang a few of the neighbours who had children Gary's age, just in case.

At last he decided that no news was bad news. Snatching up his jacket he drove round to the police station, leaving the supper congealing on the plates.

Sergeant Bowler was behind the enquiry desk, making a careful selection of next week's lottery numbers. He looked up reluctantly.

Dispensing with formalities, Robert blurted out at once: 'My son's missing. Not seen since school finished at half past three. He's out there in the dark on his own and we've got to find him. Anything could happen. He could fall over a cliff-edge into the sea or go wandering along the beach and get cut off by the tide. He could have been kidnapped or murdered . . .'

'Here, now just calm down, sir,' soothed the sergeant. 'No use getting all steamed up; that won't help anybody. What we need to do is to sort out a few details first, then we can set the wheels in motion. First off, have you got a photograph of your son?'

'No; his mother has them all. Oh, wait a minute though, there's one in my wallet.'

There was, but it was years old, having been taken when Gary was in the Infants. Still, Robert handed it over and the sergeant fastened it to a new page of his notebook with a paper-clip. Robert was just about to explain how old the picture was when the door flew open and a woman rushed in.

The woman was Janey Hunter, the one-and-only reporter on the *Sheldonsea Chronicle*. Janey was in no mood to waste precious time, for the next edition was due to go into print in a few hours.

'What's all this about a UFO taking off from the dunes, then?' she demanded aggressively. 'I'm told you're trying to hush it up. But that won't do, Sergeant. It won't do at all. People have a right to know what's happening on their own doorsteps.'

'UFO?' cried the bewildered sergeant.

'UFO?' echoed the stricken Robert, all thought of the photograph flying from his mind. 'When was this?'

He had already put two and two together and made a hundred.

Fourth Encounter
Staffroom Intruder

At that very moment, back at St Elspeth's-of-the-Storm, Gary Gardner was busy arranging a makeshift bed on the staffroom floor. He had gathered together the First Aid blanket and a huge pile of cushions, intending very shortly to snuggle down in comfort until somebody came to find him. When they did he would pretend he'd been locked in by accident and was making the best of a bad situation. He'd probably get a good telling-off, but it would be well worthwhile just to prove he'd been noticed.

He heard the telephone ringing in the

office but of course he didn't answer it. Maybe it was his dad, or maybe some other parent wanting an even more difficult reading book. Even if it was his dad, Gary needed to be seen, not heard, in the best Victorian tradition.

At the end of school that day Gary had hidden behind a huge cupboard in the television room, the gloomiest place in school and therefore the place where he was least likely to be spotted. There he had waited in some discomfort until Maggie Oates, the cleaner, had finally given a last flick of her duster and gone home. All that remained then was to fight his way through the staff-room tobacco-smog and settle down there where at least there was a carpet on which to build his bed. It wouldn't be for long. Somebody would flush him out in no time; school would be the first place they'd look. How brave they would think him, seeing his complete lack of panic!

Feeling hungry, he wolfed down half a tin of staffroom biscuits and an abandoned

banana, plus half a pint of middle-aged milk from the fridge. Then he settled down contentedly to await his rescue.

Gary didn't intend to fall asleep, but it had been a tiring day and his eyes closed almost at once. Snug in his makeshift bed, he slept like a baby.

The poor lad couldn't believe his eyes when he finally awoke to daylight and the screaming of the gulls. He stared at the staff-room clock; it was seven o'clock in the morning – but he was still here!

As if that wasn't shock enough, he noticed that the staffroom door was open, though he was certain he had closed it last night. Had the searchers been here and actually looked in the room yet failed to see him after all? You couldn't get more invisible than that!

Fifth Encounter
Hysterical Girl

That morning the hitherto sleepy coastal village of Sheldonsea made the breakfast-time news on both radio and television.

First came the account of the police search, now in full swing all along Sheldonsea's coastline, for the missing schoolboy, Gary Gardner, who was last reported to have been in contact with some mysterious stranger offering chocolates on the headland. Anyone with any information was requested to contact the police at once.

This was followed by reports of an unidentified flying object taking off from

that same Sheldonsea headland the previous evening. The authorities were anxious to stress that this was no more than an unconfirmed rumour and that there was no known connection so far between these two incidents. All the same, eager reporters were already converging on the village in hopes of the scoop of a lifetime; a scoop which might well reap genuinely astronomical rewards.

First to be interviewed by the BBC reporter was Sheldonsea housewife Mrs Vera Pratt who explained, in a state of great excitement, how she had telephoned the *Sheldonsea Chronicle* the previous evening with the first news of the UFO.

'I'd overheard some girls at the bus stop talking about these aliens on the headland,' she explained. 'Folk in silver suits offering chocolates to kids, would you believe? So when I took my dog Snuffles for a walk I kept my eyes skinned, just in case. That's when I saw this great big round thing flying over the headland. Looked as though it had just taken off, and judging from its shape it was nothing I'd ever seen before. No ordinary aircraft, that's for sure. Well, you could have knocked me down with a duster and poor old Snuffles went berserk, running round in circles and barking fit to bust, though he's not usually a barker, more of a snuffler if you see what I mean. No; I don't know who the girls were, they all look the same in them school uniforms, but if you don't believe me, go and look at the marks that spaceship's left in the dunes. Big, funny black prints, like nothing you ever saw before. Plus there was this weird scrap of paper all stuck with sand that had the word "Mars" on it twice.'

Janey Hunter, the ambitious young reporter who had received Vera's original telephone call, had already been to look. And, true enough, she did find mysterious black markings with a faintly barbecue kind of smell. Grinning wickedly, Janey had promised herself that this had the makings of the best story the *Chronicle* had run in its entire history. All it needed was the solid back-up confirmation of a few eyewitnesses.

Without further ado, Janey set about knocking on doors and accosting passers-by, encouraging folks to remember something they might have spotted, even if they hadn't made much of it at the time. She reminded one and all that they were active, interested, observant folks. Well then, surely they'd lifted a corner of the curtain at some time during the evening? Or scanned the night sky while putting the cat out or dumping the rubbish? Surely they'd noticed a strange noise over and above the telly? Or seen a weird flash of light pass through the slits in the vertical blind? Of course, it did take intelligence to put two and two together and realise what was happening . . .

'Well, now you mention it . . .'

'Do you know, funnily enough . . .'

'As a matter of fact, though it didn't occur to me at the time . . .'

It was surprising what sluggish memories Janey's diligence managed to prod. The result was a flood of amazing stories from people anxious to see their names and photographs in print; or even (glory of glories!) their likenesses on the magic screen itself.

Janey didn't mind that no two descriptions of the spacecraft seemed to tally. It was round; square; oval; star-shaped; cigar shaped; blue; bright yellow; solid gold; flashing green or blazing purple. A woman with Janey's journalistic flair could easily combine these attributes into one colourful description worthy of a world-wide scoop. By the time she rang the BBC she had a stunning tale to tell.

As it happened the world's newsrooms were facing a particularly boring set of headlines that day – nothing more exciting than drunken football fans and divorcing royalty – and were only too pleased to give this tale the benefit of the doubt. Especially since it linked up so uncannily with the missing boy, despite official denials.

Around the breakfast table at the Devines' household the radio was on for time-checks as usual, so these two items of news poured out with the Rice Krispies.

The grown-ups were only half-listening and had long since ceased to expect any really interesting titbit to have a local flavour or anything to do with themselves. But suddenly Jess Devine sat up with a jerk, gave a spluttering, gagging sound and leapt from the table, knocking over her chair.

'Choking?' demanded Jess's mother, preparing to thump her daughter on the back. 'You shouldn't eat so fast!' Then as the girl bounded into the hall she added: 'Here, where do you think you're going in the middle of breakfast?'

'Won't be long!' cried Jess, grabbing her coat. 'I've just remembered something important.'

Important was an understatement!

Before her parents could stop her she had dashed off to her friend Lucy Jones's house. That nosy Vera Pratt must have heard Lucy and herself giggling over Gary Gardner's daft tale at the bus stop. Fancy believing it! Fancy broadcasting it on the telly and letting it get blown up into this great nationwide wild goose chase! Well, it was too late to stop it now, but the two of them would be in terrible trouble if they were found to be the source of it all. So Jess needed to warn Lucy to keep her mouth shut before she gave the game away.

Sixth Encounter
A Serious Search

Gary peered anxiously at himself in the staff-room mirror. Across its middle was a picture of a uniformed zoo-keeper chasing an ostrich swallowing a pint glass. 'My goodness, my Guinness!' proclaimed the gilt words underneath. Still, Gary could just make himself out behind these ridiculous decorations.

He still existed!

This being so, he had bravely decided not to panic yet. Nothing was actually proved. Maybe the staffroom door had swung open on its own; it did have a faulty catch. So it could be that no one had thought to search the school after all, grown-ups being a lot more stupid than he'd reckoned. If they had searched the school, then maybe they'd regarded the staffroom as holy ground and hadn't dared come into it; most people daren't, especially parents.

He tried to imagine himself in the role of searcher. Where would he look for a missing boy? And suddenly the solution was obvious – he'd make a beeline for his mother's! Any child missing from a broken home was more than likely to contact a parent they hadn't seen for ages. Why hadn't he thought of this before? It was the ideal solution to his problem anyway, because his mother would notice him all right. She was the one who'd never failed to notice him in the past whenever he'd done something wrong and was actually trying to be invisible.

So that was it, he'd go home to Mum, bike, everything.

Filled with new hope, Gary searched his pockets for bus fare. Then he whooped with glee. Besides half his spends, he still had the fiver which he had forgotten to pay in yesterday for a forthcoming theatre trip. That would easily cover his fare to his mother's and something to eat as well. Quickly tidying away his bedding, he slipped out through the staffroom window and up on to the main road which ran parallel to the headland.

He consulted his watch. The morning bus was due to pass there soon. No time to reach the proper stop, but he would simply flag the vehicle down. Country bus drivers would obligingly pick up passengers almost anywhere.

Sure enough, not ten minutes later the bus appeared. Gary waved frantically at it, jumping up and down at the edge of the road. But the driver simply carried on; he didn't even slow down and gave no sign of having seen a potential passenger.

This was serious. If the bus driver couldn't see him standing alone against a clear, wide open skyline, then things were really desperate. Worse still, there wasn't another bus until the afternoon.

Suddenly Gary realised that he wasn't alone. Over on the horizon he spotted a line of men walking slowly along the headland like some bizarre funeral procession. As they drew nearer he could see that some of them were policemen in uniform and all of

them had their heads down, as though they were searching for something.

Searching for him?

On they came at a steady pace, beating the gorse and the marram grass with sticks. None of them looked up in Gary's direction. They were heading past him at some distance from where he stood, but he leapt onto a boulder and waved both arms at them.

'Hey! Are you looking for me?' he shouted. 'I'm here! I'm here!'

The nearest policeman did look up then, but with the photograph of the infant Gary clear in his mind he soon looked back again and continued his search. No time for distractions; they had a missing five-year-old to find.

As the searchers began to make their way onto the dunes and down towards the beach Gary almost wept with frustration. Why couldn't they see him? It was all the fault of that wretched key. In a sudden spurt of rage he wrenched the string from around his neck and threw the key as far as he could in the direction of the dunes, then turned his back on the searchers. Let them jolly well get on with it, then!

Now he felt very lonely up there with only the screaming gulls for company. How on earth was he going to fill in the time until the next bus at four o'clock?

Head down and hands in pockets he trudged miserably on towards the next town which was Gorston, a thriving seaside resort. At least there would be things to do there, even if it was only sitting in a shelter on the promenade.

Presently he began to notice one or two children ahead of him. Early arrivals were converging on Gorston Primary School. Gary found himself hurrying to catch them up. But these children were no better than the Sheldonsea lot. They chattered away in twos and threes and didn't stop talking long enough to notice the newcomer.

Gary managed to catch the drift of their conversation, though. One of them remarked that his friend was bunking off school today.

'What? First day of the OFSTED? Daft idiot – he'll miss all the fun.'

'Yeah, five-star day! Big chance to make or break the teachers.'

'Fancy missing that just for a session on the fruit machines!'

Fruit machines?

Why, there was the answer to Gary's problem! He would spend the day in the amusement arcade until it was time to catch the afternoon bus to his mother's.

Seventh Encounter
A Vital Clue

Police Constable Budge was hungry. They'd been searching the headland since dawn and because of the early start he'd only managed half a slice of toast at breakfast time.

'Any hopes of a break this side of midnight?' he asked his companion, Constable Fogg from the Gorston force.

'You'll be lucky!' sighed Fogg. 'Can't clock off on a job like this.'

'Yeah, I know we've gotta find the kid, but my stomach's gone on strike.'

'The thing that gets me is all this daft talk

of aliens!' grumbled Fogg. 'What will they think of next?'

'Could be something in it.'

'Huh! Daft rumours, that's all they are. When could you ever rely on eyewitnesses to tell a proper tale? Besides, it doesn't need an alien to offer chocolates to a little kid. We're dealing with something a bit more down to earth if you ask me.'

'Oh, I dunno, stranger things have happened. There was this bloke in America,' Budge remembered, 'just driving along, minding his own business when this bloomin' great spaceship came down right in front of him and these two creatures . . .'

Suddenly the sergeant's voice yelled: 'Stop talking over there! Concentrate! We want clues, not views. There's a child's life at stake here, so just get on with it.'

'Sorry, Sarge!' Constable Budge bent to his task with new determination. The sergeant was right; there was a child's life at stake, and what a boost to his career if he, Budge, could be the one to save that life!

Promotion for certain, and possibly even a medal.

Constable Budge didn't quite achieve his ambition, but he came pretty close. For all of a sudden he was startled to see, gleaming good as gold on the ground in front of him, a key on a length of string. It could well be the key to some spacecraft after all. (So many eyewitnesses couldn't all be wrong.) And if that wasn't a vital clue, he didn't know what was.

Eighth Encounter
A Run of Bad Luck

Gary eventually found himself on Gorston promenade with a stiff wind blowing in from the sea. The amusement arcade wasn't open yet. McDonald's was, though. Gary caught a whiff of burger and chips as he walked by and ravenous hunger engulfed him. He decided to treat himself to some breakfast. It shouldn't cost more than a couple of pounds and he'd still have plenty left for the bus fare. He'd never wanted to go on that boring theatre trip anyway.

He sat in a corner by the window, gazing out at the rough, grey sea and feeling suddenly desolate despite the glorious food. The girl behind the counter had seen him all right. She'd even smiled as she took his order, and had asked him if he wanted salt and vinegar on his chips. So after all, his problem wasn't invisibility; it was just that people didn't *want* to see him. No wonder they hadn't bothered to search the school! Those policemen must be looking for somebody else. The sole person he mattered to in the whole world was this McDonald's girl, and that was only because he'd paid her with his five-pound note and she was hoping for a big tip from the change.

Well, he'd show them all! He'd *make* them care. He wouldn't go to his mother's after all; it was far too obvious. There were plenty of alternatives. He could stay on the bus all the way to the terminus at Brackfield, a busy city where there were all kinds of exciting things happening. He could have a real adventure there, seek his fortune like heroes in all the best stories, and maybe never go home again. Come to think of it, he needn't wait all day for that afternoon bus either; he could take any bus to anywhere. Or any train. The more he pondered, the more reckless his plans became.

At last, having demolished every scrap of his breakfast plus half a muffin and two sugar-lumps abandoned by a previous diner, he set out for the travel Interchange. He would study both bus and rail timetables there before making up his mind where to go.

On the way he had to pass the amusement arcade. Well, his time was his own, so why not spend a few minutes in there after all? Perhaps he could hit a jackpot, replace the cost of his breakfast and even make enough for the fare to somewhere truly special, like London? Nobody would ever find him there, and serve them right!

Gary handed over a pound at the change kiosk then walked round jangling the coins in his hand as he surveyed the machines and wondered where to start.

One machine in particular took his fancy.

It had a moving platform full of tenpenny pieces. He stood and watched as a man rolled another tenpence down a chute. This new coin shot into position at the back of the moving platform, pushing some of the other coins forward. These in turn pushed others, until a whole cascade of them dropped over the edge of the platform and into the prize-winning cup.

What a glorious sound and an even more glorious sight!

Gary stood open-mouthed, watching a small fortune clatter into place.

The lucky winner scooped up the coins triumphantly, filled his pockets and went whistling merrily on his way, wise enough to quit whilst ahead.

It was a doddle!

Gary immediately took the man's place and began feeding in his own tenpenny coins. Each one shot into position and pushed other coins forward all right, but unfortunately not a single coin dropped into the cup. All the ones likely to fall had just

been collected by the previous winner.

At this point Gary remembered a boring maxim one of his teachers had repeatedly preached – 'If at first you don't succeed, try, try, try again!' He ran back to the kiosk for another pound's worth of change. Then another. And another.

With feverish concentration he fed the coins in one by one. He couldn't stop now, for it was surely just a matter of time before there was another great cascade of cash, most of it his. He had made an investment in this game now, and couldn't possibly give up without a win.

Then suddenly he felt in his pocket for the next coin and realised there wasn't one. His pocket was empty. All his money was gone, every last tenpence. He was broke!

How on earth had that happened?

Puzzled, resentful and alarmed, Gary gave the machine an almighty kick. That certainly dislodged a few coins, but it also dislodged, from his corner office, Mr Bullock the manager, a tough-looking man in a brown overall with a long string of machine keys festooned around his waist.

Before Gary could lay hands on his illicit 'winnings' Mr Bullock had him by the scruff of the jacket and was hauling him towards the exit.

'Out you go! We don't want any cheats and troublemakers in here. You're under age anyway, and why aren't you in school?'

'Let go of me!' yelled Gary, trying to twist himself free. But Mr Bullock kept a firm hold on him and began to frog-march him forward. Gary launched himself into a desperate struggle during which he accidentally kicked Mr Bullock much too hard on the shin. The manager howled with pain. Letting go of Gary, he clutched at his damaged leg, staggered backwards and fell, catching his head on the corner of a fruit machine. Blood gushed from somewhere above his ear as he lay quite still with his eyes closed and his cheeks turning a deathly shade of grey.

Somebody screamed. It was the woman from the change kiosk who had seen the manager fall. She dashed over, took one look at the blood, then rushed to the nearest telephone to summon an ambulance.

Gary was horrified. For one terrible moment he stood rooted to the ground. The man was obviously dead and he, Gary, was a murderer! He saw that people from all parts of the arcade were beginning to close in on

him, anxious not to miss the excitement. He had to get away! Suddenly the adrenaline began to flow and Gary took to his heels before anyone could stop him.

Once outside the arcade he ran recklessly along the promenade, dodging or colliding with the growing crowds of holidaymakers.

He had reached as far as the pier before he was obliged to pause for breath. And there ahead of him was an eerie sight. A strange figure was beckoning to him – the same squat, silver figure he had seen on the Sheldonsea headland a lifetime ago. As he watched in horror, the figure began moving towards him, calling some message from which Gary could just make out the one word 'spaceship'.

Ninth Encounter
A Broken String

Robert Gardner stared at the plastic envelope which the sergeant was holding out to him. Yes; that was the door-key-on-a-string which his son usually wore round his neck. Robert compared it with his own key for extra confirmation.

He found this a very upsetting moment, for the string hadn't just worn thin; it had been violently snapped. Had some villain wrenched it from the boy's neck before he . . .? Not daring to think any further than this, Robert subsided moaning onto a chair and the sergeant ordered someone to fetch

him a cup of hot, sweet tea. But as soon as the poor man was feeling calmer the sergeant cast sympathy aside and began a sharp interrogation.

Wasn't the lad a bit young to be a latchkey child? And was Mr Gardner aware that it was against the law to leave a child so young in the house by himself?

Knowing he was in the wrong, Robert

began to bluster. He explained about the arrangement with Mrs Flyte, adding rather too hastily that Gary needed to slip home now and again, probably to fetch some book or other to help with his homework.

'Homework?' cried the sergeant. 'But he's only in the reception class! They surely don't get homework at that age?'

This was the moment at which Robert remembered the out-of-date photograph and began moaning all over again.

Tenth Encounter
A Dusty Bed

Gary Gardner had never run so fast in his life. That silver figure really was an alien after all. What's more, it seemed to be stalking Gary who was too upset to wonder why nobody else was taking flight. The poor lad left the promenade behind and turned inward towards the busy shopping centre of the town.

He decided he would have to stop running soon or he would collapse in a breathless heap, but where could he hide?

On a sudden impulse he dashed into the first big store he saw and leapt on to its escalator. It seemed wisest to leave the street as far behind as possible, so he rode straight up five floors to the very top, which proved to be the home of bedroom furniture.

Desperately scanning the possibilities of somewhere to lie low, he scuttled down the aisle between rows of beds and finally squeezed himself into the gap between a king-size headboard and a massive wardrobe. Crouching there on the dusty floor he was able to see only the feet of passers-by. But he guessed that would be sufficient to spot the enemy. Suddenly a bedknob came rolling by him so he pocketed it to avoid discovery. Then it was time at last to confront his desperate situation. Amazingly he found that his whole attitude had changed. Now that he was a murderer, and hunted by aliens as well as the police, he wished only to become invisible after all. It seemed the advantages of going unnoticed far outweighed the pleasures of being the centre of attention. If only he had realised this in time! If he had stayed at Gran's in the first

place and been contented with his lot, none of this would have happened! Or maybe his big mistake had been to throw away that magic key! Now he was on the run and it was only a matter of time before he was spotted.

Time dragged on agonisingly slowly. There didn't seem to be anyone around; beds were not exactly selling like ice-cream in a heat-wave. Years seemed to have passed before Gary heard voices approaching. Heart thumping, he held his breath to listen. Then he saw three pairs of feet: two male, one female. One pair belonged to the sales assistant; the others to a couple who were hoping to buy a bed.

Gary was obliged to listen to a long, boring discussion of the merits of various mattresses. Then a sudden cloud of dust arose as the male customer threw himself on the bed to try it out.

'Come on, give it a whirl!' he urged his companion.

So the female customer sat on the edge of the bed.

As she moved around trying different spots the dust situation worsened. Gary held his nose and prayed. He might sneeze at any moment.

Eventually the movement stopped and the

missing feet reappeared. But then the woman wanted the assistant to lift up the mattress so that she could examine the base of the bed.

More dust!

That did it! From behind the bed there erupted one almighty sneeze, followed by a grubby boy who flung himself at fantastic speed towards the down escalator. As he did so, a bedknob came bouncing from his pocket.

They had flushed out a shoplifter! The assistant whipped out his mobile phone and spoke to one of the plain-clothes store detectives. As a result, the detective was waiting for Gary as he stepped off the second escalator.

Eleventh Encounter
A Weird Balloon

Jess Devine and Lucy Jones decided they had better find Gary Gardner before this whole weird situation landed them in a load of trouble. After all, they were the ones who had unwittingly started the 'alien' rumour which was growing out of all proportion. Folks were actually saying now that Gary had been whisked off in a spaceship.

'I'd never have believed grown-ups could act so crazy,' sneered Lucy. 'Even my mum reckons she saw a spaceship zooming past when she was closing the bedroom curtains.'

'Grown-ups will do anything for a nice,

juicy drama. Look at the way they turn up in droves to gawp at every plane crash or motorway pile-up.'

'It's disgusting.'

'All the more reason for us to get a move on.'

The police didn't seem to be having much success, so the two girls bunked off school and set out themselves to track Gary down.

'Suppose you were Gary. Where would you run to?' mused Jess.

'As far away as possible. I'd be fed up with everything, especially being dumped at a new school with no friends and no mum.'

'Yeah, he hasn't even got a dog. We could have been a bit nicer to him I suppose. He must've wanted to be friends since he was yakking on about giving us chocolates.'

'What if he's gone back to his mum?'

'Not likely. It's too far, and anyway his mum would have said something by now. He wouldn't have had much money, so I'll bet he's walked over to Gorston thinking he could easily hide away among the holiday crowds.'

'Come on then, what are we waiting for?'

The girls began to walk along the coast road following Gary's earlier footsteps but were soon halted by an unnerving sight. Something that looked like a small silver spaceship was hovering over them.

Gasping with horror Lucy clutched Jess's arm, but Jess began to laugh.

'It's only a balloon! A big one though, made to look like a spaceship, landing pods and all. Very clever.'

As she spoke the balloon floated down to earth and bobbed along the grass verge in front of them. Jess chased after it.

'See? That's all it is. It's covered in luminous paint which must be what everyone caught sight of. I guess it would've looked pretty spooky sailing along up there in the moonlight.'

'Don't touch it!' cried Lucy suspiciously. 'It could be poisonous or explosive or something.'

'Get a grip!' sneered Jess. 'You've been

watching too many videos. I can even tell you where it comes from. You know Masquerade, that theatrical hire shop that's been having a closing-down sale? They had a load of "Star Wars" and "Doctor Who" stuff they were trying to get rid of. Not just costumes but props as well. Come and look, it's got their logo underneath.'

Lucy stayed put and Jess sighed.

'Honestly, can't you recognise a balloon when you see it? I happen to know all about that sale because my dad threatened to buy us this Dalek they had in the window. He said if we stood it behind our glass front door it would do a better job than a burglar alarm. Come to think of it, I bet what Gary Gardner saw on the headland was somebody wearing a space-suit they'd just bought at Masquerade's sale.'

'You reckon? Giving chocolates away as well?'

'Well, maybe he made that bit up.'

Lucy moved closer and stared at the balloon. She had to admit Jess was right; it

had all the markings and protrusions of a well-imagined spaceship, yet it was nothing but a toy, a shapely bag of air that could no doubt be demolished with a pin.

'Well, you can't be too careful,' she said in her own defence at last.

'I'm being careful.' Jess cradled the object tenderly in her arms. 'Come on, we'd better take it to the police right away. The sooner we scotch all those daft rumours the better.'

'Here, not so fast! We can't go bursting into a police station before half past three or they'll know we've bunked off school. Our folks could get taken to court and fined or something.'

Jess rolled her eyes. 'Aren't you a prize-winning Misery Guts?'

'Besides it'll be even better if we track Gary down as well, then we'll be heroes instead of villains. I'm right, Jess. We've got to keep on looking for him.'

'Oh, all right; but only until half past three. And you'll have to take a turn at carrying this thing.'

Twelfth Encounter
A Heavy-handed Detective

First thing that morning police officers had turned up to search Mrs Flyte's house, but she wasn't there. Mrs Flyte had made a rare trip into Gorston to have her hearing-aid repaired.

The old lady decided this was a good opportunity to do some shopping, so she happened to be in the same department store as Gary during his episode with the bed. Better still, by a lucky coincidence, she happened to be at the foot of the fourth floor escalator at the moment when the store detective took his warning call and sprang neatly forward to lay hands on the suspected shoplifter.

Because of her faulty hearing-aid Mrs Flyte had not been listening to the news. She knew nothing about the police search for the missing boy, but she recognised Gary at once and was outraged at the rough treatment he was receiving.

'Leave him be, you great bully!' she cried, aggressively waving her umbrella. 'That boy ain't never done no harm to nobody!'

The store detective ignored her and continued to manhandle Gary, whereupon the old lady lost her temper and used her umbrella to strike the man a nasty blow on the shoulder. With a howl of pain the detective let go of his captive to clutch his wound, and Gary scuttled free.

The terrified lad was out of that store in seconds while Mrs Flyte rallied a crowd of supporters who barred the way, making sure the store detective could not follow. There was soon so much noise and confusion and general obstruction that the manager

turned up, demanding time-consuming explanations.

All this gave Gary a chance to flee back towards the promenade where the crowds were thickest. He had some wild notion of heading for the pier where, if the worst came to the worst, he could dive off the end and swim under water, hoping some friendly paddle-boat would pick him up and whisk him away to France.

This and other fantasies began to take over his brain. In fact, the whole episode was becoming a nightmare, for there ahead of him once more was the weird silver figure, this time with a couple of spaceships floating just above its head! Gary was being stalked, or haunted, or both!

This new shock made Gary veer away in the opposite direction. He dived down a side street, then another and another, until he ended up at the rear of the amusement arcade, though he didn't recognise its back view. Just as he was feeling totally lost and confused he heard his name being called. Then, one shock piling quickly on another, his arms were seized by a couple of girls who turned out to be Jess Devine and Lucy Jones.

Now Gary's panic turned to anger. These two could see him perfectly well after all. They had always been able to see him. So this whole disaster was their fault. If they hadn't sat giggling over that comic and pretending he was invisible, he would never have needed to go into hiding in the first place.

'You two stupid idiots! You know what you've done?' he spluttered, red in the face. 'You've made me kill somebody!' Gary was beside himself with rage. Yet furious as he was, he couldn't help thinking it felt pretty good to have somebody else to blame.

'You what?' laughed Jess, thinking this was some sort of joke.

But Lucy asked, 'Is that why you ran away?'

'Take no notice,' Jess told her. 'How could he kill anybody, a weedy scrap like him?'

'I have, I tell you! He's dead! There was blood all over the place.'

'Who's dead?'

'This bloke who looks after the amusements, the one in the brown overall with all the keys round his waist.'

'Oh, you mean him?' said Jess, pointing across the street to where Mr Bullock in a bloodstained brown overall was emerging from the back of the arcade. As they watched a woman waved him into his car but not before she had taken charge of his long string of keys.

'Yeah, that's him!' agreed Gary as it slowly dawned on him that the man wasn't dead after all.

Thirteenth Encounter
A Prodigal Son

Mrs Gardner heard the news of her missing son at breakfast time and was instantly distraught.

She rang up her husband at once.

'What's happened to our Gary? What've you done to him?'

Robert did his best to explain but really there was nothing helpful he could say. The police were getting nowhere.

'Believe me, I'd do anything to find him! I've been searching all night. I'm nearly out of my mind with worry. I feel so helpless, stuck here all on my own.' His voice was shaking with emotion.

Mrs Gardner began to feel sorry for him. 'Don't you upset yourself, Robbie, you're not on your own any more; I'll be right there! We'll track him down between us; two heads are better than one.'

She jumped into her car and drove off at once, stopping only to call at the supermarket to cancel her lunch date with Mr Slopton.

That certainly caused an upset. Mr Slopton's face collapsed into a childish sulk.

'But you can't cancel! Not today! I've arranged something really special,' he whined.

Mrs Gardner was disgusted.

'Nothing's half as special as my Gary,' she snapped, 'and if that's all you care about my missing son then you can jolly well eat both lunches yourself, and I hope you get terrible indigestion.'

She had suddenly realised how much she was missing Gary. She should never have let him out of her sight. Now he was in danger

and it was all her fault. It could already be too late to make amends. How upsetting it must have been, she thought guiltily, for the boy to be uprooted and dragged off to the seaside away from all his friends. No wonder he'd run away.

'If anything's happened to that boy I'll

never forgive myself,' she told herself as she prayed desperately for him to turn up safe and well.

It seemed her prayers were answered. For as she drove along Gorston promenade on her way to Sheldonsea her car suddenly screeched to a halt. Startled holidaymakers watched in amazement as she leapt from the driving seat and flung herself in the path of heavy traffic, risking life and limb as she dived across the road to where a boy was being frog-marched along by two girls.

'Gary!' she yelled at the top of her voice. 'Stay there – don't move! And you two just let go of him before I call the police!'

Mrs Gardner careered forward, scooped up her son and swung him joyfully in her arms.

'Oh, Gary! Are you all right, son? Your dad and I have been frantic with worry.'

Gary said he was fine, and he meant it. For if he wasn't a murderer after all, and if his family cared so much about him, then nothing else mattered.

'What happened, son? Did these two kidnap you, or what?'

'No, we didn't!' cried Jess, outraged. 'We just rescued him.'

'He was being chased by an alien,' added Lucy. 'Didn't you see it on telly?'

'Shut up, Lucy!' hissed Jess who didn't want to hear another word said about aliens ever again.

'You mean he thought he was. He has a vivid imagination, my Gary.'

'No; it's true. We even found this balloon, only it was too big for us to hold on to and it blew away.'

'What a tale! Still, I should have been there for him, if only to tell him what a silly idea that was. He could have frightened himself to death!'

Squeezing the breath out of Gary in a punishing hug, Mrs Gardner added: 'You know, son, all this has opened my eyes. It's made me realise how lost and miserable you must have been feeling. I should have thought of that sooner. I know this sounds even dafter than your aliens, but it's as though I was bewitched and the folks I really cared about had turned invisible for a while. But I can see them now all right. It's going to be different from now on. You're coming back home with me.'

'What about Dad?'

'He can come as well, if he wants to. I must say I've missed having him about the house.'

'No more keys round my neck?' asked Gary.

'Never! I promise! I'll be in every day when you get home from school. Now come on, we'd better put your dad out of his misery and show him you're OK.'

'Just a minute before you rush off!' inter-

rupted Lucy cheekily. 'Don't we get a reward for rescuing him?'

Mrs Gardner smiled. She was so happy at being reunited with her son that she felt well-disposed to everyone.

'Yes, why not?' she said. 'There's a big box of chocolates on the back seat of my car. You can have that, and welcome. I've gone right off chocolates all of a sudden.'

About the Author

Hazel Townson was born in Lancashire and brought up in the lovely Pendle Valley. An Arts graduate and Chartered Librarian, she began her writing career with *Punch* while still a student. Reviewing some children's books for *Punch* inspired her to write one herself. Over sixty of her books have so far been published and she has written scripts for television. *The Secrets of Celia* won a 'best children's book' prize in Italy and *Trouble Doubled* was shortlisted for a prize in the North of England. She also chairs the selection panel of the Lancashire Children's Book of the Year Award. Hazel is a regular visitor to schools, libraries and colleges and her books have been described as 'fast-moving and funny'. She is widowed with one son, one daughter and four grandchildren.

The Speckled Panic
Hazel Townson
Illustrated by David McKee

When Kip Slater buys *truth*paste instead of
*tooth*paste, he and his friend Herbie soon realise
the sensational possibilities of the purchase.
They plan to feed the truthpaste disguised in a
cake to the guest of honour at their school
Speech Day but, unfortunately, the headmaster
eats the cake first . . .

'A genuinely amusing quick-moving story'
British Book News

ISBN 0 86264 828 9
paperback

Rumpus on the Roof
Hazel Townson
Illustrated by David McKee

Mr Bunch is disappointed in his un-macho
son Harry. Yet Harry is the one who tracks
down the villains threatening the old lady
next door. And in the end it is Harry's
undersized physique which proves to be
the only thing that can save the situation.

'Racy, entertaining stories typify Townson'
Books for Keeps

ISBN 0 86264 591 3
paperback

Disaster Bag
Hazel Townson
Illustrated by David McKee

Colin Laird is seriously worried about the state
of the world. Disasters are happening all
around him, and he decides to acquire a Disaster
Bag filled with all the equipment he might need
in an emergency. Only then does he begin to
feel safe. But how could he possibly guess that
a terrorist would slip a bomb into his bag when
he wasn't looking . . .?

'One of Townson's best'
Books for Keeps

ISBN 0 86264 524 7
paperback

Ignorance is Bliss
Hazel Townson

Amy Bliss and her cousin Harry meet on a
train, each on their way to seek help from
their grandmother for frightening personal
problems. But Gran already has problems
of her own and the journey turns into a
nightmare of panic and misunderstandings.

**'Hazel Townson tackles the sticky problem
of a little knowledge being a dangerous thing'**
Observer

ISBN 1 84270 042 1
paperback